First published June 2016. ISBN-13: 978-1533428905

Printed by CreateSpace, An Amazon.com Company

Front cover: Peter Megoran

Jim Ferguson

A South Sea Adventure

To great uncle Phil, thanks for letting us stay. Enjoy the read...

By Jamie Megoran

Love,

This story is dedicated to my teachers at Archbishop Runcie First School, Newcastle-upon-Tyne.

Acknowledgements

I would like to thank Abi Thomson and Rachel Megoran for proof reading this book, as well as Peter Megoran for drawing the cover illustration. I am grateful to Nick Megoran for helping me publish it, and Emily Megoran for encouraging me and introducing Carly into the story. My dog, Molly, was the inspiration for Belta.

Contents

Table of Contents

Chapter 1: The *Golden Dolphin*

I had been sitting on the barrel for at least an hour, and had already eaten half a dozen apples. The waves were rising and crashing down on to the harbour-side. As I lent on the crate beside me, I watched everybody getting more and more tired as they heaved on board the good ship *Golden Dolphin* gallons of rum, caskets of fresh water, animals, rope, personal cases, and sacks of money, weapons, and crates of dried fruits, biscuits and salted meat. I wondered how this little ship would make it across the oceans with all this heavy load without sinking. If I had known what would befall this ill-fated voyage, I would never have agreed to be the ship's boy.

About ten minutes later a tall man with a short moustache walked up to me and tugged me roughly on my collar. 'Come on Jim-lad,' he said sternly, 'it's time to get on board.' I could not refuse, since he had a knife, a cutlass and a gun all hanging off his belt. Shyly, I walked on board not knowing what adventures would befall me. 'Oh, just by the way,' added the man, 'my name's Arthur Scarface, I'm the bosun. You'll do as I say.' I didn't imagine he would be my best friend on this voyage! As my feet touched the gangplank, I had this horrible feeling I'd never see Ireland again.

I was awakened from my thoughts when a small black dog bounded up to me licking my legs. 'Get lost, Belta!' yelled the bosun as he kicked the dog out of the way with his big, black buckled boots. The dog yelped as it was thrown against a hard, cold cannon. She fell over on her side and got back up again her tail between her legs and you could see by the expression on her face that she was confused and frightened as if to ask *'why did you do that, what did I do wrong?'* I rushed off to her side and stroked her. The dog slightly wagged her tail and gave me a little lick, but when I stopped stroking her,

her tail drooped down again. I felt sorry for her and beckoned her to me, and she came. 'Good girl, Belta,' I said gently. I realised that with a little bit of practice I could train her to be extremely clever.

Suddenly a short, fat man shouted, 'Get ready to set sail!' After he said this, two thin men turned a giant wheel which winched up the anchor. I peered over the deck, staring at the greeny-bluish water. Slowly but surely the harbour was moving away from us; or were we moving away from the harbour?

By mid-afternoon the land was now almost out of sight. I decided to have a sleep before the launch party that was planned for that night. I was woken by the slobbery feeling of the dog licking my face. I checked the clock – it was half past eight, and the party was at half past nine. I decided to get up now, and go to the lower deck to see if I could help move anything up to the deck. It was already dark, and so out of a cupboard I took a lantern and lit it with matches. Other people were asleep, so I had to tiptoe through the dark corridor. I turned left and then right until I came to a flight of stairs. I pulled the handle and pushed the trapdoor open. When I was on the deck, I could see in the dim light that people were getting ready for the party. There were three men carrying seats, and two more heaving the captain's mighty oak chair. Other people were rolling barrels across the deck, and unpacking containers. A grand table stood in the middle with a white table cloth on it. People were laying the table with fine plates and cups made from china. A place right at the end of the table was set with golden cutlery. I guessed that would be for our captain, Ben Hawkins.

A man was standing smoking his pipe and leaning against a staircase. He looked like he had nothing to do so I came up and asked him, 'Can I help with the party?'

'You can fetch some lanterns, Jim boy, from the ship' store,' he said in a rough tone. I replied, 'okay' and tiptoed back down the stairs. I wasn't very sure where the store was, but I decided I'd just explore the ship more and thought I would eventually find it. I crept through the corridors making sure I didn't wake up anybody. After a long time of hunting around I found a door with a sign above it saying, 'SHIP'S STORE.' The handle was rusty so it took a bit of jiggling, but I soon had it opened. I found myself in a passage with large boxes leaned against the sides, plus cages of chickens and barrels of wine. They were all tied up with string, and I had no idea which one would have lanterns in them. After a search I found a box with a label saying, 'FRAGILE, LANTERNS.'

As I walked up to it, a black shadow moved among the boxes. I felt scared – what was it? I took out my little pistol from my pocket and aimed at where it had come. Two more shadows quickly went by, and I decided it would be no use trying to get it with the pistol. I brought out my penknife and the next time a shadow came I attacked it. I missed on the first strike, but the second time I got it. When I lifted the shadow out of the darkness I saw a rat impaled on my blade with blood streaming out. It writhed for a few seconds, and then it stopped. I went to the back and took out a trolley to carry the lanterns on. With all my might I heaved the box onto the trolley and pushed it back out of the door.

Instead of returning the way I came, I decided to explore the ship a bit more so I went through a long corridor. There were about 20 doors leading off. But there was one thing which really caught my attention. It was a noticeboard pinned right next to a door saying 'NAVIGATOR'S ROOM.' The noticeboard looked like this:

JOBS:

HAWKINS, Ben	CAPTAIN
MANATEE, Carl	ASSISTANT CAPTAIN
IRONSIDE, Tom	NAVIGATOR
SCARFACE, Arthur	BOSUN
GRIND, Samuel	ABLE SEAMAN
CAPUCHIN, Andrew	ABLE SEAMAN
THIN, Steve	ANCHORMAN
MARMOSET, Harry	ANCHORMAN
THOMPSON, Jude	CHIEF OF ARTILLERY
MACDONALD, Simon	ARTILLERYMAN
SMITH, John	ARTILLERYMAN
ERIKSEN, Erik	ARTILLERYMAN
LACROSSE, Pierre	ARTILLERYMAN
FERGUSON, Jim	SHIP'S BOY
LEMUR, Frank	SHIP'S BOY
MARTYN, Henry	CHAPLAIN
DeQUINCY, Marmaduke	SURGEON
DOVE, James	LEADER OF MELEE COMBAT
DOOL, Leo	MELEE COMBAT
SHARP, Jason	MELEE COMBAT

WILLIS, Archie	MELEE COMBAT
ROBSON, Ainsworth	MELEE COMBAT
ROBINSON, Sir Charles	SCIENTIST
FRANKS, Tommy	LOOKOUT
GREYWATER, Finn	COOK
GIBBON, Chippy	COOK'S ASSISTANT
ALSOP, Andrew	DECK-HAND
CHIMP, Jude	DECK-HAND

I read this for a few minutes, until carrying on down the corridor. When I got to the stairs, I asked a scraggly-looking young man, who it turned out was the Frenchman Pierre Lacrosse, for some help. Together, we heaved the case of lanterns up onto the deck. When I looked around, the party was set up with barrels, a big table, small tables, and even a man practising a fiddle for the dancing.

I sat on a box of dried fruits for about half an hour, and in that time more people came from the two doors under the staircase to the poop deck. The party eventually got underway: there was feasting, drinking, laughing, singing and dancing to the merry playing of the fiddle. At one point Tommy Franks got so drunk he fell off the deck and into the sea. I guess he must have drowned because he was never seen again. But soon everything was back on track. The party was a jolly ending to the start of our voyage. Little did I suspect that our voyage would not have a jolly end.

Chapter 2: Fire!

The next three days of our voyage passed well. Solid old Finn Greywater and cheeky young Chippy Gibbon cooked us good food. Sea-wizened Ben Hawkins captained us carefully, demonstrating the experience he had gained from all he had been through. Tom Ironside navigated skilfully, and everybody else did their jobs very well. It seemed like there was nothing to stop us from reaching our goal, to circumnavigate the world. The only thing I had to be wary of was the Arthur Scarface's temper, and Frank Lemur's bullying. Frank was older than me and jealous that I had been allowed on the ship so young.

On the fourth night of the voyage I went to sleep early, after Jude Chimp, the deck-hand, showed me how to play the fiddle. I had a pleasant sleep, but woke up at 1.30 sweating and hungry. I went down to the galley to ask for some food, for Finn Greywater or Chippy Gibbon were always awake. When I got to the wooden door I noticed something strange. Faint wisps of smoke came out from under the door. I decided to continue to find out what was causing this. I swung open the door and a dreadful sight met my eyes. There was the cook's assistant, Chippy Gibbon, asleep in an armchair, his pipe still burning. Not only that, but half the armchair and half the room were burning too! Clearly his pipe had set fire to most of our food supplies, and spread from there. I crawled under the smoke coughing and spluttering trying to get to Chippy. I shook him frantically trying to wake him up. 'Chippy, Chippy wake up, you're in danger!' I yelled. I wiped the ash off his face, but it didn't make any difference. His sapphire eyes were tight shut, he was dead. He was doomed, and so was the ship.

I tried to crawl away but was overcome by smoke, and collapsed on the ground. It seemed impossible to breathe, as smoke filled my lungs. I tried to get away but it was no use as fire was circling all around me. I felt life was slipping beyond my grasp.

'What's up, what's up?' I heard a voice screaming. Sir Charles Robinson, our expedition's eminent scientist, rushed into the room. 'Help,' I pleaded as loud as I could, and although it only came out as a whisper, Sir Charles heard me. He dragged me out of the flaming room. My first breath of air came in, I felt life slipping back into me. By this time, people were surrounding me and others were yelling. Leo Dool called for the surgeon, Marmaduke DeQuincy, and he helped me back up. John Smith and Erik Eriksen ran past me down the corridor with buckets of seawater and threw them into the cook's room. But it was no use as the flames had now spread into other parts of the ship. We were doomed.

Meanwhile, on the deck, men were getting ready to lower little boats into the sea to escape. I scrambled up to the deck trying to reach them but the final one was already leaving and Harry Marmoset shoved me out of the way. I fell back and banged sharply against an empty barrel of rum. I got back to my feet and tried to jump into the boat, but it had already been launched and I fell into the water. The sea was freezing and I tried to swim but the current pulled me down towards the deep, dark depths below. Just then I looked through the water to see Belta franticly trying to get to the surface. I grabbed her, and tried to push her upwards. I opened my mouth to try and breathe but horrible salty water filled my stomach. I was thrashing the waves trying to save myself but it was no use. Through the blur of the water I could see a boat sailing past but I knew I would drown if I didn't reach the boat. Just as I was about to run out of air I felt a tug on my leg and was pulled back to the surface. 'You owe me something for that, little monkey rascal,' said Andrew Capuchin. As the boat pulled away, I just managed to get Belta in.

As I looked up again I could see the ship aflame, and half was already under water. Another boat pulled alongside ours and they were so close together it scraped my back. I was surprised by the pain, and fell back into that boat. Belta bounded after me. Sir Charles Robinson asked with concern, 'You okay lad?' 'Yes,' I murmured, but I don't think he heard me, because something caught his attention. The ship was gone.

Chapter 3: Out of the Frying Pan, into the Fire

We were cold and wet, but everyone had managed to escape into the boats, apart from Chippy Gibbon and artilleryman John Smith, who had perished in the fire. Tom Ironside, our navigator, told us that there were some inhabited islands about 50 leagues to the west. For the next few hours the journey was quite peaceful and cheerful, because the men knew they were going to be rescued on the islands. Steve Thin, Harry Marmoset and Simon Macdonald were chatting away while having their rations of biscuits, salted meat, rum and fresh water. Sir Charles and Jude Chimp were playing cards like children, and Leo Dool was tending those who had been injured.

A small breeze was blowing, but I noticed it was slowly getting stronger. I decided to have a little nap so I could be fresh when we got on the island. I fell asleep peacefully at the stern of the boat. I was awoken about two hours later by Simon Macdonald shaking my shoulders. 'Wake up! Wake up!' he cried. I looked around. Huge waves were crashing into the sea and some of the other boats. On a boat near to us, Jude Chimp had been knocked into the water and was splashing frantically trying to get back in. I felt terrified, sure that we were all going to drown in this fearsome storm.
On another boat, Jason Sharp was pointing to the horizon and yelling. I looked up and through the raging torrents could make out the dark shape of land about a league away. People's hearts leapt, but the question was: could we make even this short distance through the terrible storm?   We all pulled hard on the oars, straining to reach safety. We were getting closer with every pull.

Suddenly a 10 foot high wave reared up behind our little boats, getting higher and higher every second. Through the blur of the water a flash of orange showed for a second, but then the wave crashed. I closed my eyes, expecting to drown, but when I opened them our boat was being thrown back on the after-pull of the wave. I looked back at the boat, and everyone was sodden. But I couldn't see everybody, because it was covered by a giant orange octopus! Its prehensile tentacles were writhing into the air and crashing back into the little boat. I was terrified, it felt like I was looking at an enormous dragon. I could see Frank Lemur coiled up in one of the octopus' cruel tentacles, with bits of his body getting thrown everywhere. Then the Octopus leapt over into my boat, capsizing it, before attacking the next boat and throwing it up into the air. I took another breath as I pulled myself back up to the surface of the water, but then everything went blank.

Chapter 4: Landfall!

I woke up to the sound of waves crashing in front of me. My body was soaking wet from head to toe. I lifted my head and looked around, and saw that I was lying on a large, sandy beach a mile long. In the distance huge cliffs rose above my head, and it looked like they touched the sky. Behind the beach there were enormous pine trees with birds' nests jammed into the dark trunks. I could just make out the enormous shapes of large mountains, towering in the horizon. In between the forest and the mountains there was a grassland of flowers. But the most amazing thing about it was the animals. A few wild boars were lolloping in a mud-pool just in the sand-dunes. Huge birds flew everywhere, and it felt like I was the first person on earth. I named this island 'Frelser', Danish for 'Saviour,' which was a word Erik had taught me on the voyage. I offered God a prayer of thanks for my survival.

I stood up and looked around hoping I would see somebody. At first I couldn't see anyone, but then I saw the shape of another person about 50 metres away lying face down on the beach. I ran over to him shouting, 'Can you hear me?' I was terrified. Was he dead, or was he not? If he was, then my chances of survival alone were pretty low on this remote island. His fine clothes had now turned into soggy rags, and had blood all over them. His eyes were closed, and there was no sense of movement on his body.

The person stayed still for a second, then lifted his head. I tried to get a picture in my mind of the noticeboard in the ship, and then I remembered – it was Jude Thompson, with that gloomy face, but who always had a twinkle in his eye. 'What happened?' he asked in his gruff Irish accent. 'Errrrrm -,' I mumbled, 'well we're stuck on a remote island in the middle of nowhere.' His face went white, then pink, then white again in surprise. He leaned over and vomited out sick and blood. He coughed two times and then threw up again. It was a gory sight indeed. I daren't say anything.

'Food,' muttered Jude desperately, 'and water! There's plenty of it around us.' I looked around thinking he was joking, but then I realised he wasn't. About 20 metres away a few barrels and a couple of containers had been washed up on the shore. He looked at the boxes again, then back at me, smiling. 'Looks like we gotta bonus chest, ain't it?' he joked. I laughed, but it wasn't really a laugh, as I had just been stranded on a tiny island in the middle of nowhere.

We found out that the sand-dunes were bursting with things from the ship. We found two trolleys and heaved them on with all our might. It took a long time to do this because we found gallons of rum, caskets of fresh water, chickens, rope, personal cases, and sacks of money, weapons, and crates of dried fruits, biscuits and salted meat. It looked like we wouldn't starve on this island – for a while, at least.

'What do we do now?' I asked. 'Well, what would *you* do?' he responded. 'I dunno,' I replied in a rather shamefaced tone. 'Come on, think!' he replied.

'I would make some shelter, but...' I started, 'But, you're hungry!' he interrupted sharply. 'Well, yes,' I said again. We sat down in the sand-dunes and had a small meal of dried meat and water.

We wondered where we should look to make our shelter. We knew what we would make it out of – the remaining sails of the ship. 'Let's just build our shelter here on the beach,' I suggested, feeling tired. 'Haven't you read the Bible – the foolish man built his house on the sand,' joked Jude. We decided to head to the plains, and heaved the heavy load through the sand dunes and the forest. This wasn't easy as the trolley wheels kept crashing onto the hard tree trunks, making the loads wobble. At one point it wobbled so much that everything on my trolley fell off and we had to put it back on again.

It took about 5 hours to get there, by which time it was mid-afternoon. We both slumped down onto the soft dirt. After having a 15 minute rest we got back to work, and went over to a small hill where we decided to build our house. The hill was only 40 feet wide and 20 feet high, and we started building at a flatter surface. We got part of the mast and stuck it into the soft ground below, and did the same with another part of the mast parallel to it. That was the easy bit, the hard job was getting the sail over. The wind kept trying to blow it away up to the top of the mountain, so we had to keep on going back and getting it down. Eventually the thing was finished, making a small shelter. We put our belongings inside and next to it, and strung up two hammocks between the posts. That was all we could manage on the first day, for it took a couple of hours and after that we got into our hammocks and fell asleep as soon as our heads touched the ropes.

I woke up in the night with Jude shouting at me: 'wake up, quick, now!' he yelled. I looked around. Lightning was all around us, forking down like giant arrows. The roof of our tent had completely flown off, blown away in the wind. Rain sloshed down all around us. But Jude wasn't interested in that – he was pointing up to the top of the nearby mountain. I looked up, but couldn't see anything. A crack appeared in the rock, and boulders were tumbling down towards us, smashing everything in their path. 'It's an avalanche!' screamed Jude, 'run for it!' He said that just in time. We jumped away to see a rock the size of my head whizzing straight past us. More rocks came, and we retreated into the jungle for protection. I hid behind a large sycamore tree which I thought should protect me. But Jude was not so fortunate. He stumbled through the jungle looking for a place to hide, but just before he could get behind a thick tree, a rock smashed right into his sandals tripping him over and making him fall to the ground unconscious.

I ran out, but this was a risky move because just then another rock rolled past us. I leapt back into my tree, before the thing crashed past. I then came back out again, and dragged Jude by the heels behind the tree – just in time, because then a sharp chunk of rock came past and banged into the trunk of our tree. It groaned, and started to topple. I heaved Jude away behind a stronger-looking oak tree, as the sycamore crashed down to the ground.

Our first night on the island was not the best of all. But it was not about to get easier any time soon.

Chapter 5: Falling!

Over the next couple of minutes the avalanche became less violent. Within 20 minutes only occasionally a small rock or pebble travelled past. Jude was still unconscious, although I listened to his breathing and realised it was at the correct rate. When it safe to step out again, I sat Jude up against the tree and went back to the place on the mountain where we had left our stores. I knew Jude would want a drink when he came round.

Surprisingly, only a couple of the barrels and containers had been damaged by the avalanche. I checked the labels of about five barrels and eventually found one with the word 'RUM' painted on, but not very clearly because a stone had scraped the sides. I opened it up, but realised something strange. Instead of my hand getting fully wet when I pushed it in, only my fingertips did. I peered in to see about a gallon and a half of rum, instead of the usual four gallons. At first I was shocked – how did all of that rum get out? Then I realised – just above the level of rum there was a small hole broken into the dark wooden sides. I frantically checked the other barrels, and to my dismay realised that although we had lots of food, almost every one of the barrels with water or rum in had been holed. This was bad news – if we didn't find a source of fresh water soon, we would die of dehydration in this intense sun!

I rolled the only sealed barrel of water back to Jude. When I reached him, I found that he had come to, and was standing up. He looked at me and said, 'where have you been?' I told him all about our dire shortage of liquids, and this made him look sick and worried. I gave him a few drops of water, although only a bit so I could save the rest when it would be needed. He didn't say anything for about 20 seconds, and then he murmured under his breath, 'A new shelter, we've gotta make one, ain't we?'

'We'll sure need better shelter,' I replied, 'but first of all we must find water. No point making a nice home if it'll only become our grave.'

Then Jude walked over towards the hills and mountains whose snow-capped tops went straight up into the bulgy clouds. I was about to ask him where he was going but he didn't look like he wanted to be asked, so reluctantly I followed him along the muddy grassland marked by patches of pink, white and red flowers as tall as me. Eventually, I asked him where he was going. He pointed to some 50 foot high hills made of dark grey rock with a few flowers and shrubs growing through the dark cracks. I started saying, 'But there's no wa...' but 'we'll find some somehow,' interrupted Jude sternly. I dared not say anything so I followed him for the remaining distance to the hills, when he told me he wanted to go to the top of the hill alone. I sat down on the dark grey rocks with thin brambles running over them. Just as I was getting settled, I felt the ground under me giving way, and I was falling down into the earth! I tried to grab onto the rocky side, but it was no use – I was falling further and further, deeper and deeper. Eventually, I reached the bottom with a splash – I had fallen into some freezing pool or river. I went under, and was terrified, splashing and flailing with my hands. I gasped for breath, but my lungs only filled with water.

Suddenly, I came back up over the surface. I coughed and spluttered, and stood up – it was only waist high in what seemed to be a clear, slow-moving underground stream. I felt dazed and sore, but luckily nothing seemed broken. I yelled for Jude, and then started looking around for a way back up, but I could barely see anything. Up above I could see the clear sky through the hole in which I had fallen. Although I couldn't see much, I could hear perfectly – I heard a bat fly around what was evidently a large cave. As my eyes slowly adjusted to the dark, I could make out that there was a vine hanging down from the surface where I had fallen in. if it wasn't too slippery, I could probably climb up it with no trouble at all. I grabbed hold of the vine, and started to go up.

At first it was easy, but half way up it started to get very slippery. Suddenly I fell. I clung on the vine to save myself, but it was no use. I slid back to the bottom of the rocky cavern. I started up again. This time, I avoided the slippery bit and climbed up the other side of the cave, where there were ledges I could put my feet and hands on. After a while I heard Jude shouting from above, 'Jim! Jim! Where are you?!' He reached down and helped me up the last bit, and sunlight hit my eyes. 'At least we've found a water source, young man,' remarked Jude smiling, 'but next time don't jump straight down into the well!'

We followed what we thought might be the downhill slope of the underground river for some time, hoping that it would emerge in an open spring. But after an hour of wandering around we couldn't find anything. By now we were getting hot and very thirsty, and desperate for water. In the end we decided to use the hole as our well, lowering down a bucket from the wreck on a length of rope. The water we drew up was cool and fresh – now we knew we would not die from dehydration. We decided to name our well, 'The Saving Well,' because we had been about to die from the immense heat.

Chapter 6: Our home

Our next priority was to find shelter, for we did not want a repeat of last night. This time we decided to make a stronger shelter from the thin slabs of granite which were contained in the ship. I went to get some mud to use as cement, while Jude dug a small trench in the ground. We then filled it with the wet mud to make the foundation for the building, and put the slabs into the trench, every time sticking them together with mud.

Our next problem was a roof. We had nothing to use, and the slabs were not long enough to provide shelter over the top. Also they were so heavy that they would probably fall down on us straight away. Instead, we decided to take apart couple of barrels and use the wooden planks for the roof. It took a bit of work, but eventually we had about ten long planks which we then fitted over the top. Because of the shape of the barrels, our roof had a slight curve which would be great for draining away the rain. Then we had to make a door, from some of the planks left over from the roof. We were clever enough to leave space for the door, but the sky was already turning pink so we had only a few minutes before night. However, it became hard to work because both Jude and I were feeling pangs of hunger. We went into the forest to forage for fruits, and I found pomegranates and bananas. Jude found grapes and coconuts. For the first time on the island we had a decent meal and fresh water. But still we had to make a door. It was quite dark now, but luckily Jude had made the wooden part for the door (but not the hinges). I made a carpet from the sails, and also strung up two hammocks, made of torn sails, between the walls. When I finished this, Jude showed me the ingenious solution to the problem of how to hang the door without hinges. He attached ropes to the top of the wood, then fastened them to the roof with granite weights. We could push the door and come in or out, but an animal like a fox definitely couldn't get in. We called our new home 'Hillside House.'

After all of this it was night time, so we climbed into our hammocks and I found a lantern from the wreck and lit it. After a while I blew it out, and we both immediately fell asleep.

Chapter 7: An unexpected reunion

Our second night on the island was definitely better than the first one. When I woke up late in the morning, Jude was still fast asleep in his hammock. I lay there listening to him snoring, and thought how strange it was that the two of us should be trapped alone together on this island when we had such different personalities. Jude was a determined and funny man, who always tried to make jokes in the worst of times. Although he was a natural leader, he could be unpleasant to me when he bossed me around. I, on the other hand, was quite an anxious little chap, and perhaps the best word for me was timid.

After thinking about this for a little while, I woke Jude up. He told me today we would go exploring, and improve our home with possibly a chimney, so we could build a fire for cooking inside. He first told me to go to the beach and see what food and drink resources I could find which had been washed up from the wreck, while he started work. I wandered along the beach and dunes, feeling the sun's scorching brilliance around me. I found lots of food, but only five barrels of drink. I also came across tools, weapons, a clock, a hose, and packets of money which weren't very useful to us now. I decided to bring these back to Hillside House, then see if I could find anything in the jungle. Jude was pleased with my find, but said it wouldn't last very long, so I went into the jungle with a rifle and a lantern, because evening was falling and the big leaves blocked out lots of the light.

As I was returning I heard a rustle in the undergrowth. The rustling got closer – it was clearly an animal – yet I couldn't see anything. I was terrified – I thought it could be a serpent or some giant cat, or a dangerous species of predator which had never been discovered before. I stepped back – still it got closer.

I stopped. I froze. I was petrified.

I was too afraid to get the rifle out of my belt. I tried to scream to Jude for help but not a sound came out. The animal got closer – it was practically upon me. I took one step back, and another. My lantern hit a branch of a tree and went out. Suddenly, I turned and ran, in the darkness. The animal ran – the chase was on. I was going so fast that in my panic I did not see a root from the great acacia tree and before I knew what was happening I was sprawled on the ground. Suddenly, when I thought my life must be over as the beast would get me, a slobbery wet tongue licked my forehead. I looked up – and saw the brown and white of Belta! I was so relieved my heart missed a beat. I patted her and stroked her, and she gave me lots of licks all over, as she leapt about in pleasure. I was pleased to have company so I made up a list of what was good about having Belta on the island:

REASONS WHY I'M HAPPY FOR BELTA TO BE ON THE ISLAND

1. I have company
2. It will be easy to hunt with her
3. She will be good on lookout
4. She can round up animals and get them closer to us
5. She will protect us from wild animals

She walked with me as I took the stuff back to our new house. "Well, looks like you got us a pet as well," remarked Jude when we got back. "You'll have to train and look after her," he added. Because I knew Belta from the voyage, I was sure it wouldn't be too hard to do this, so I accepted this. He also showed me an extension he had added to the house. With a pickaxe recovered from the wreck, he had started to mine into the rock which was mainly made of soil and stone. For the next few hours I helped him with this. We placed our stores in the cave so they were safe from any rain, and then Jude suggested an amazing idea. He said we could use the rock we had mined out to make a wall around our home and the well.

Later in the day when Belta and I were out hunting, we shot a young deer and brought it back for Jude. We gathered enough wood to make a campfire, and over it roasted the deer on a spit. It was a lovely meal, for we had fruits to begin with and each shared part of the deer, gave some to Belta, and left the rest aside for tomorrow. We drew water out of our well, which was lovely and fresh. It was almost like having a roast meal but without the potatoes. Our meals on the island were just getting better and better.

Chapter 8: Building a new life

When I woke up the next morning we decided we were going to work on the wall. Jude said he would start mining into the rock to get more materials we needed, and he told me to mark the ground where the wall would be built.

It was a very hot day, but I set to work as Jude had told me. Firstly, I made a mental list of stuff we would need to be protected. This was the well, the fireplace, and our home. I found some flint lying around. I used it to mark a long line in the ground to show where our wall would stand. It was hot and tiring work, but Belta always kept me company. After a couple of hours of work I returned to Hillside House. I found out that Jude had cleared out a huge amount of space in the rock, and just outside the door there was a big pile of sand, mud and rock towering above me. At about mid-day we had some of the leftovers of the deer, and some fresh melons and coconuts which I had picked from the jungle nearby. After we had a nice lunch I was refreshed and ready to get back to work. We started making the wall together, using the mud and sand as cement to hold the chunks of rock together. Over the next few hours I noticed how our mountain of sand, dirt and rock was turning flat, and eventually ran out when we were about two thirds of the way. At this point we decided to stop for the day, for the sky was turning pink and orange. We ate what was left of the deer and the fruits, and I ran over to our well to draw some fresh water. I flopped down onto my hammock and almost immediately fell asleep, with Belta curled up beside me.

In the morning I woke up and the sun was shining all around me. I could hear Jude working right at the back of the house, and for the first time I actually felt comforted. Jude had made our home lots nicer with no more ridges on the walls. Furthermore, he had split the back of it into two rooms – the store, which was the one I could see, was filled with barrels, boxes and sacks, so you could barely walk through it. But I managed. When I eventually got to the end, Jude had made a wooden wall with a hole which I had to bend my head to walk through. There I saw Jude's project – a little boat. He showed me what he had done, but he also told me he had made a passage out to the other side of the hill so he could get the boat through there out to a lake he had seen in the distance. He showed me where the passage was, and I asked him why it was so high. 'Well, you didn't think the boat wouldn't have a sail, did you?' He told me he was going to make some gun holds to fit our rifles through in case any wild beasts tried to attack us. Apparently, he couldn't sleep and had been working all through the night and was going to work on this for the rest of the day, but said he would rest at noon when it was too hot to work.

"Meanwhile, you can work on finishing off the wall," he said. "I've left a big pile of mud and rocks for you to use, just through the passage." After he said this, I went down through the long, dangerous passage – for it had lots of spiky rocks sticky out from the sides, walls and even the roof – but I managed. When I got back out into the sunlight I was so relieved I thought that passage would never, ever end.

I had to close my eyes for I was not used to how bright it was, even though Jude's tunnel was small, it was dark. I looked around trying to find the pile of rubble, but I couldn't see it anywhere. So I shouted through the tunnel 'Jude! Where did you put the pile?' Far away, I could her a feint voice 'up the top of the ul.' What on earth was 'ul', I asked myself? And then I figured it out – he meant hill. When I found the pile, I pushed it all back down to the bottom and started on the wall. It took me many hours to finish it, but I eventually did, keeping a space for a gate. I also found a little stream was running into our ground, which gave me an idea – maybe we could grow food?

Together, we had made a comfortable and safe home.

Jude finished it off by flying an English flag he had found in the wreckage from the top of a tall pine tree growing by Hillside House. He told me it was to attract the attention of any passing boats who might rescue us. I had a terrible feeling that it might instead be an enemy who saw it first.

Chapter 9: We are not alone

Three seasons passed, and life on our island had become quite comfortable. Our house was nice and warm, for we had made a fire and a chimney which opened at the top of the hill. We had found more furniture from the wreck, including tables and chairs, plus lots of other useful items. Our wall had been finished, and cannons were placed there for defence. With the stream, we had irrigated the land to make a rather large allotment. We found some seeds on the wreck, but most we had gathered from the island although we didn't always know what they were. We were growing wheat, carrots, potatoes and garlic, and a delicious vegetable we had found that looked like lettuce. We had herded a few wild boar which we could eat. Jude had also tamed an eagle he named 'Flash', so hunting was a lot easier with an eagle and dog, as Belta had turned out to be a fine hunter. Jude and I were both missing home, but we had got used to our new lives.

Hillside House was built overlooking a river, which was about four miles away. One day we followed the bank of the river north, for we had already orientated ourselves to the ground. On the way we noticed wild grape vines growing. This meant that, when they were ripe, we could collect the grapes to make wine. Many monkeys were climbing around the trees, screaming at us and throwing sticks if we got too close to their territory.

After travelling for about ten miles the river opened it into a surprisingly large lake, which we guessed was the source of the river. We had a rest on a sandy beach alongside. My hands were so tired after carrying all of our resources, I pushed them down into the soft sand to relax them. To my surprise, after going down a few inches the sand wasn't soft at all, it was more of a rock. I felt my hand round the stone, which seemed like a perfectly smooth oval. I pulled it out not realising what it was, and stuck my hand back into the sand –

there were many more rocks, all the same. Then Jude exclaimed, 'I say, you're bringing out turtle eggs!' He helped me scoop them all up – there were dozens. 'Omelettes tonight for us!' chuckled Jude. It was too late to head home, so we spent the night alongside 'Turtle Lake', as we named it.
In the morning we fried some of the turtle eggs as we didn't have all the ingredients we needed for omelettes. As we walked along the beach Jude stopped suddenly and exclaimed in alarm, 'Look, footprints!' Sure enough, there was a line of human footprints leading from the jungle, to the shore and back. This meant we were not alone on our island. We followed the footprints which had sort of skimmed a lot of sand everywhere, so I guessed somebody must have been running. We were terrified – was this an angry tribe whose land we had invaded? We crept along the trail from the beach, and then I saw a column of smoke rising from deep in the forest. As we made out way towards it, these were probably the scariest moments I had had on the island.

We were so close. I was trembling with anxiety. I saw a spear rising above the bushes. Suddenly Belta sprang forwards, and the man yelled and fell to the ground. We came over to look at who it was, ready to defend ourselves if attacked, but Belta was wagging her tail and licking the stranger all over. It was Tom Ironside, the navigator of *The Golden Dolphin*! We greeted him warmly and shared our stories of survival on the island.

Tom told us that, on the night of the shipwreck, he had clung onto a barrel until it got washed up on what we had christened Turtle Lake. He had made a den with a blanket and lit a fire outside. "It was cold and wet and miserable," he told us. At the end of his long, terrible story about being attacked by wild beasts, trees falling on his den and no food for days, plus being very, very lonely, he said that he would definitely like to live with us. We told him our story, and he seemed very impressed at our new life as we told him of our survival.

We set off back to Hillside House where Tom fell asleep almost immediately after having a drink of our fresh water. Jude and I had a little meal first. I put up another hammock and had a rest, while Jude went back to working on the finishing touches on his boat.

Chapter 10: The Great Expedition

We soon settled down to life with the three of us. Tom was pleased to have company and proved very good at gardening and growing crops. We decided we would like to know what the whole of our island of Frelser looked like, and explore it. This was when Jude's boat came in handy. It could fit five people in, although they would be super squashed. It had a short mast with a little sail, and although it would not be safe in the open seas, we hoped it would be enough to take us round the coastline – or out to a passing ship for rescue if we saw one come near our island. If indeed Frelser was an island – which we still were not sure about.

To take the boat from our home to the sea, we chopped down tree trunks and used them as rollers. This took many hours and was hard work. It was my job to bring supplies for our expedition while Tom and Jude moved the boat. Eventually we rolled it all the way down to the river that led to Turtle Lake. We launched the boat, which we named *Explorer*, and it was an anxious moment wondering whether she would float properly. I was to be the first person aboard. We made a gangplank out of thin wood – it was creaky, but at least it worked. My foot lifted a step on it, and as it touched the wooden surface the boat wobbled but it stayed afloat. You would never believe how relieved I was.

Once we had put all the supplies board, we set sail south down the river. We passed a barren island at the mouth of the river, and turned East along the shore where we had first landed. We went past some cliffs and called them Lookout Cliffs, because they would make great places to see what's coming towards us. We then sailed past Landing Beach. We glided past a bay were we saw shark fins coming out of the water, so we named it Shark Bay. We advanced around the headland with a tiny little island at the bottom of it, then headed north up past a beach. Turtles were crawling around so we gave it the name Turtle Beach. We dropped sails and rowed up to the beach, where we had lunch. Belta barked and jumped around the turtles, but they ignored her.

Tom went into the forest at the edge of the beach to explore. We suddenly heard him shouting. Grabbing our rifles we ran to where he was, thinking maybe he was getting attacked. But when we got into the clearing, he showed us what he had found – no enemy at all, but lots and lots of sweetcorn. He was very excited, and we helped him gather corn to eat and to grow. We also found some strange purple fruits with soft centres and leaves that looked like dragon's tails.

We made a fire on the beach and grilled some of the corn for lunch, before continuing our voyage up the east cost of Frelser. We were about half a kilometre off the coast, which was now grassland, and seemed to be filled with animals and birds. We could see two mud pools where the sand met the grass, with wild boar lolloping in one of them. I was the first person to notice this, but after about 12 miles of travelling we were drifting further and further away from the coast. I pointed this out to Tom, who said he had noticed it too. We all realised we were getting pulled out by a current. We got the four oak oars Jude had made, but it was no use. It seemed like the harder we tried, the harder the current tried. Eventually we saw the shape of another, much smaller island ahead of us. But Tom and Jude weren't looking at that – they were watching the grey fins that were swimming menacingly towards us.

Chapter 11: Sharks, seals and penguins

We all grabbed the oars and rowed fiercely, but that was no match for these sharks. They were circling us. The first attack battered the boat. Tom shoved an oar at the next shark which lunged at us. We were getting closer and closer to the island, but could we reach it before the boat was sunk? Jude took a harpoon we had salvaged from the wreck, and tried to attack the sharks – sometimes we won and sometimes they damaged the boat in a desperate battle. Belta crawled into a corner whimpering. The shape of a dark grey shark leapt out of the water towards us. Jude and I dodged it, but Tom was hit by the powerful fin and was knocked down with a crunch into the hull of the boat. It chopped off the whole mast with one bite of its huge jaws before splashing back into the water. Our situation was looking grim, but we were close to the shore – could we make it? Suddenly there was a massive jolt and we were turned upside down for a few seconds. When the boat righted itself, we were all sodden but the sharks weren't following us now as we were so close to the rocky shore. We crawled onto the beach and pulled the battered boat up after us, collapsing with exhaustion. Belta shook the water out of her coat and flopped down next to me. But we were safe.

The windswept island we had landed on was about two miles square and was mostly rock and sand, with a bit of grass poking out in places. When I had caught my breath, I drew a map of the coastline we had seen so far, remembering to add in the names we had given island parts. We decided to explore this barren island. We could see penguins everywhere. They were all Rockhopper penguins, and there must have been thousands of them huddled together, so their squawking was very loud.

Behind some rocks there were no penguins at all – they had fled from three huge, grey leopard seals. If we could catch one, we could use the pelt for winter clothes, eat the meat, and use the blubber for wax in candles and oil in lamps. We crept up behind it with our guns and Tom's harpoon ready. Tom whispered '3…2..1..GO!' We all shot, and Tom threw his harpoon. The largest seal screeched, and fell down dead while the other two slipped into the sea.

While Jude repaired the boat, Tom and I chopped the body up into parts – meat, blubber and the pelt. We then hauled the parts to the beach and loaded them into the boat before continuing with our voyage. We named this rocky island 'Penguin Island.'

I was anxious as we set off, but Tom and Jude were now prepared for the sharks when they came back. There were lumps of seal meat to distract them, plus the rifles were aimed into the water. We could see the first sharp coming clearly. We threw a chunk of meat, dripping with blood, behind us and rode furiously towards the sand banks where the sharks wouldn't follow. As soon as it scented the blood it lunged straight at the seal meat, and other sharks quickly came and fought for it. When we had left the sharks behind us, we could see great, snow-capped towering mountains on the north of Frelser, stretching into the clouds. The foot of the mountains were stuck into lots of iced-over marshes.
It was about half an hour later when we noticed it was getting colder. We were sailing along the north coast of the island now, and we named the mountains 'The Great Mountains' because they were the biggest we had seen on Frelser. The beach was made out of spiky rocks with icicles hanging down. At the back of the beach was a layer of thick snow.

Behind one rock there was a mountain of ice, but then it moved down under the rocks. We were all shocked, and sailed closer to get a good look. We could see an arctic hare walking around in the snow. But suddenly a great, sort of white cat leapt onto it and caught it. It was a snow leopard! Its fur looked as soft as velvet – it was a silvery, greyish colour

The Great Mountains

with beautiful white teeth, which now had rabbit fur in them. Its eyes were glinting in the sun. This sleek animal walked majestically through the snow, leaving a trail of pawprints. I stood admiring it. Tom aimed his gun at it, preparing to shoot, but I was so angry I smacked the gun down out of his hands, and it went off with a bang, the bullet shooting into the water. At that noise, the animal roared and disappeared. 'What did you do that for?!' Tom shouted. 'No, what did *you* do that for?' I argued with him, 'I'm not going to let you harm a beautiful creature like that.' Tom looked grumpy but shut up.

It was getting dark now and I attached a lantern to the front of the boat so we could see our way. We eventually came to the mouth of a river, so we sailed into it and travelled upstream. On our left were the great mountains we had been sailing along, but on our right it was very different. There was a great savannah with the occasional dotted acacia tree coming up in places. Each bank of the river was made entirely out of mud, with shrubs growing here and there. After sailing down the river for at least an hour the mountains on our left had turned into grassland, with the odd hill. We then came to a mouth of another river running into ours, and as far as we could see it flowed down from the Great Mountains which now looked to us like blobs of rock in the distance.

We decided to camp at the mouth of the river, but just as we were about to jump onshore we saw hundreds of salmon fish gliding through the water. We reacted quickly. Belta was the first animal to attack, and Flash was next, shooting down to the water with his claws pointing down and coming back out with the catch. Tom, Jude and I tried to lure the salmon to the beach and Tom made them jump out of the water and onto the bank where we had made a pile of at least 20 salmon. The chase had finished within a minute. We were all sodden and tired, but at least we had a good catch. I made a fire to cook the fish, tossing a couple to Belta and Flash. Tom went out exploring to see what he could find, and Jude found a pool of dried rock salt which he used to salt the leftover fish to preserve them for later.

When Tom got back he was grinning. He lifted up at least five bunches of grapes. We had a lovely meal with grilled fish and grapes. We also got some containers from our little boat which we had anchored from the shore and put the remaining grapes in. Tom remarked, 'How about we save some of the grapes to make wine?' Jude agreed to this idea at once. I didn't really say anything because I was thinking about what other things we would find. After the meal, Jude told me to get some more grapes but bring a barrel this time so we could get as many as possible. I guessed why he said this: he just wanted to make wine! It was a lovely spot, and we named this new river 'The Running River.'

The map I drew on our expedition

We set off down the main river again. It got wider and entered a wide lake. On the left side of the lake the shoreline was a straight beach, with mountains close by. The right side was curving into the dry land surrounded by jungle. Suddenly I thought: hadn't I been here before? Wasn't this the place we had found Tom, and all the turtles were crawling up the beach? Or was this just similar? "Hang on," I said, "don't you recognise this place? Wasn't it where we found you, Tom?" Tom definitely said he recognised it. "Then," I said, "if that's correct then this lake is what we called Turtle Lake, but really it is actually a bay and we have just sailed all the way round our island!"

Jude remarked, "And if that's right, then everything on what we thought was the right bank of the river is another island, and quite a dry one, which we haven't explored!" I got my map out. Firstly I drew the new things we had explored. Secondly, I had to rename 'Turtle Lake' 'Turtle Bay,' and I named the two islands 'Eastern Island' (which we had just sailed round) and 'Western Island' for obvious reasons.

The rest of our voyage was not so eventful. We started sailing around Western Island, which was mainly desert and savannah but with a jungle oasis by Turtle Bay. A day later we sailed back to the place we started from, and took our haul of grapes, sweetcorn, seal pelt and meat, and salted fish back up to Hillside House. It took us two trips to do that, and when we had done that we had a long rest. I lay in my hammock finishing off the map. As I fell asleep, I thought about our three day voyage and that although we had many resources, we knew we were truly alone in a great ocean.

Chapter 12: Canine Chaos

The next morning was a warm day with only a slight breeze blowing. After having breakfast (turtle-egg omelette) we had a rest before Jude and Tom came into our bedrooms announcing that they were going to make canoes for us to explore the channel separating Eastern and Western islands and go up the running river. Jude said that he and Tom were first going to store away the stuff we had got from the expedition, while I went out with Belta into the jungle to search for bamboo for the canoes.

After crossing the hills for at least half an hour I started to enter the forest of flowers next to the side of the jungle, which was ringing with noise: birds squawking, monkeys screeching, and insects buzzing. There were also some scary sounds of unseen mammals roaring. After about five minutes venturing into the jungle, we found the first stem of bamboo. It seems like it went into the clouds, it was so tall. I swung an axe into the bamboo, which made an enormous creaking sound before the bright green tower crashed to the ground. I only really needed two before my bags would have got filled up, so I chopped them down into smaller pieces and took them back the way I had come.

After a long and tiring journey I got back. Jude and Tom seemed impressed with my find. They started working on the canoes, while I went back to gather more bamboo. As I approached the bamboo growing ground, I heard a frightful roar and a terrible screech. I got down and crawled through the thick flora towards the clearing where the sound was coming from. I pushed away leaves the size of my foot and saw a terrible sight. Four great leopards were tearing apart the carcass of a panda, roaring and cackling as they did it like a bunch of mad hyenas. Then, a twig cracked under my foot and they instantly turned to look at it. It was a moment of horror. The leopards were snarling with their yellow fangs looking devilishly horrible. Suddenly one of them sprang towards me. I only had seconds to react. I instinctively snatched my emergency pistol which was deep inside my pocket. Just as I lifted it up, the thing leapt at me and knocked the pistol out of my hand. I was thrown down helpless, with a sharp pain in my wrist. I screamed in terror, thinking the end had come.

Just then I heard a loud BANG and a screech of pain. I looked back to see a great wound in the leopards' side. It was probably the first gunshot ever heard in that jungle. The leopards fled with terror and the birds immediately flapped their wings to get out of the place. Out of the bushes came Tom grinning. 'Thank you,' I said, 'you saved my life. How did you get here in time?' 'I just came to help you get some more bamboo,' Tom replied. 'I heard the noises but when I came over you were on the ground. I hoped I'd hit the leopard and not you!.

We were distracted by the sound of a bleating noise. A pathetic baby panda was pawing what was obviously its dead mother. I took a few steps towards it. It didn't even notice me, just kept on whining like a person knowing he's about to die. We decided to take the cub home, and it clung to me tightly like I was its mother now.

When we got back to Hillside House, we saw an almost finished canoe. I wondered where Jude was. I went to our bedroom to find him lying perfectly still on the floor. I panicked: was he dead? Flash was sitting quite calm on some jutting rock as if nothing had happened. The table was stained with something red – was it Jude's blood? But suddenly I found the answer – on the back of the table there was a pile of grapes. It was obvious – Jude had started making wine and got drunk. We were used to this, for he had got drunk many times on the good ship *The Golden Dolphin*.

Chapter 13: A surprise in the Western Island

A fortnight later both our canoes were ready and we decided to use them to continue our exploration of our home – especially the Western Island. Tom and I were in the first canoe, while Jude paddled furiously in the other. We headed west and went round the whole island in a clockwise direction, but there was nothing but desert in the south and savannah in the north. We saw gazelle, and a mud-pool with some young rhinos wallowing. We made camp for one night and tried to hunt a gazelle but we failed because they were so fast. We shot a snake that threatened us, and roasted its meat and made a nice warm scarf out of its skin. We ate some of the stores Jude had before setting off again.

Our journey was peaceful until we reached Turtle Bay where we could see two logs in our way, floating on the surface of the shiny, blue water. Jude was a good canoeist and steered around them. But Tom and I had not so much practice, and just as we thought we had made it the back of our canoe hit the front of the log. Immediately it came alive. It crashed into our canoe and turned us upside down. The front of the log opened showing rows of sharp teeth – it was an alligator! I tried to find the surface of the water with my hands so I had to move to the side before clambering onto the upturned canoe. The water was freezing. But where was Tom? The water turned red – was Tom all right? I knew he was a good swimmer, but no-one can outswim an alligator. There was lots of blood in the water now – surely he would faint, and be left helpless. I looked anxiously over the water but I couldn't see anything. Every now and then the tail of an alligator thrashed the surface of the water. Where was Tom? I was desperate. Suddenly his head burst up through the water. 'Grab my hand,' I shouted, 'but just as he was about to he was pulled back under. By now, Jude had come over to help me. The good thing about these canoes was that they had two sitting compartments in each, and Jude had used his spare one to store ammunition. He pulled out a double-barrelled rifle, and when the crock's tale appeared again he fired! There was a bang, a swish, and a splash, before the alligator sunk down into the water never to be seen again. But was Tom lost with him?

Neither of us said a word. Everything was silent. Just below the surface a turtle swam by, his greyish-green shell rising from the water. Everything was silent and sad – it seemed even the animals were. There was no way we could save him now. He was lost. We sadly started rowing to the shore. Just then I felt a strong jolt under my canoe. 'Oh no!' It was probably another alligator – a very hungry one. The jolt knocked me into the water, but just as my head was about to go under the surface of the water, I could see Jude smiling. I started swimming away, but felt a tug at my leg.

It was Tom!

I pulled him into my canoe, and we rowed to the shore of Western Island, where we decided to set up camp at the edge of the jungle and Jude told us about what had happened. He said that the blood was not his, but the alligator's, because Tom had a knife in his belt so could fight as well as the alligator. We lit a blazing, red fire and roasted a wild pig Jude had trapped, before going to sleep.

I woke up to hear rustling in the undergrowth, I nudged Tom awake. 'What's that?' I whispered, pointing to the place where I heard the noise coming from. Suddenly, I was astounded to see a human face appearing! It was a young girl around the age of 10 or 11. Luckily she hadn't seen us. She was picking bananas from the vines which were growing in the jungle around the beach. I was too surprised to move or speak.

Suddenly, Tom gave a grunt of pain as the wound from the shark attack stung badly. The girl spun round to look at us. She was almost as surprised as we were. Then, a boy appeared out of the bushes as well. He looked about 13 or 14, with long unkempt hair down to his neck. For a few seconds everything was silent. Silence was worse than speech. Then a gruff voice sounded from the undergrowth, 'who's there?!' All at once a man, around the age of 35, burst out of the undergrowth. He had a big moustache and beard but short, untidy hair. All three of them were wearing creamy white shirts which, were torn and dirty. Their trousers were rags. I heard the boy whisper to the girl, in a frightened voice, 'Is this the Spanish again?'

Chapter 14: Acquaintance in the jungle

After the girl had got over the shock of seeing us, she walked calmly over to Tom and took a bottle of white liquid out of her pocket. She lifted his head up, and poured a few drops of into his mouth. Was this poison, I wondered? Tom recognised the taste of medicine, so she was clearly a friend who was trying to help us. The girl turned and smiled at me: 'Carly,' she said in a soft, relaxing London voice, 'the name's Carly. And you're not the Spanish, are you?'

'No,' I said, 'we're from Ireland but our neighbouring country, England, is at war with them.'

'So you're not the Spanish?' she said again.

'No,' I repeated. 'Last year we set out to make a new colony but our ship caught fire and we escaped in small boats. We tried to row away but a storm struck us and we three were the only survivors.'

'Whoa,' she said, 'our ship was wrecked by a storm my dad, my brother and I were washed up here. We've been here for about two years and we still haven't found our mum Beatrice. Have you seen her?' she asked anxiously.

'Not that we know of,' answered Jude, 'but although we've sailed round both islands we haven't explored everything inside.'

'Oh,' she whispered, then her father stepped in. 'Just to let you know, the reason we're hiding in this jungle, even though it's not a great place to live, is that we are afraid of the Spanish. They've come here before and we thought they might come again.' 'I'm pretty sure you can move out now,' exclaimed Jude. 'I know the Spanish. If they only come once a year they probably won't come again. We haven't seen them from our home.'

'Are you sure?' asked the boy, whose name was Hugo. Hugo gave Belta a big cuddle. She was very pleased, and took a quick liking to him.

'Yes,' I replied. 'We've got pretty good defences – a few cannons, and a strong home with quite a lot of room, so you could move in.' They were extremely pleased at that offer. We all set off home carrying our canoes back down to the bay. They had a lot of storage which they wanted to take, so they had to go in two journeys to bring it all. They hadn't got much from the wreck, but they had new clothes which they had created from furs, plus spears and swords they had made. They also had hundreds of tools they had made, and lots of rope which may come in handy. We had to make a number of trips across the channel carrying all their food, items and of course the people, but eventually we were all there and set off back to Hillside House through the hills.

They had two hammocks with them and we had an extra one, and we hung them up in an empty room we had hollowed out recently, alongside a small table and a chair. They settled in surprisingly quickly.

A few days after the new family came into our life, Carly's dad, whose name was Finn, suggested that we add more defences. I hadn't thought about that much, we had a few cannons and a wall which I thought were enough. But Finn said they'd be nothing against the Spanish. After this, Tom liked Finn very much. It was him who suggested cool mechanisms of defence, so three days later we had already added a long trip-wire all the way around the wall which activated bows and arrows. Over the next few weeks we built two large watchtowers, each of which had two floors and a balcony. By the time we finished that, Jude and Finn had already started working on the next project – another wall surrounding the tripwire. We also dug out a tunnel which went right under the defences, and came out just next to a stream with a large stone you could cover up the entrance with. It was also sealed with a wooden board which had leaves and soil stuck over it for camouflage.

This all took around five weeks to do, and when it was

finished our defences seemed indestructible. Sooner than we thought, they would be tested to their limits.

Chapter 15: Chase or battle

Most people think a walk in the bushes is a healthy way to exercise. But in fact, it isn't always – actually, it could be life-threatening. I discovered that today.

One evening, as I walked by myself around the rocky lookout cliff overhanging the great blue sea that stretched off into the horizon, the seagulls flew overhead squawking and screeching. Below me was the long yellow beach, the sand of which was glittering in the sunlight like pearls. Tall thin trees stretched up high into the sky before arching out to form a roof-like canopy. The light-rays shone through the forest ceiling, casting shadows on the dark flora below. The bright green leaves sprouting out of the ground reflected the sunlight so much that it looked like somebody had splashed them with golden paint. The ground was covered with hundreds of tiny mushrooms, plus scattered groups of snowdrop-like flowers. Occasionally, I came across a large plant with purple flowers sprouting abundantly out of them. They were covered with beautiful butterflies, different types of swallowtails we only dreamed of seeing in Ireland.

The point I am trying to make is that this place was wonderful. Maybe my life here wasn't so bad after all.

It was only when I fully came out of the forest and stood on the edge of the cliff that I saw them. They were enormous. It didn't seem like they were moving at all. Seeing these things was like having a black spot placed into my hand, but worse. The front of them was covered with golden patterns. I froze when I saw them.

They were three Spanish galleons.

I crouched in the bushes to hide so they didn't see me. By this time, it was late evening and I had a drink of warm water from my water bottle. It was nice and hot as the cold of evening fell. I crawled along the ground trying to keep undercover in the tall, green palm branches. The last of the sun was disappearing over the horizon. Eventually I reached the edge of the overhanging cliffs, overhanging some more cliffs, which overhung the sea.

I slowly and carefully edged my head over the cliff so I could see clearly down below. And what a sight I saw! Dozens of small tents were pitched on the ground with their white pointy pyramid-like tops standing against the night sky. Night had now fallen, but not a star could be seen. In the centre, a huge flag stood like a giant tower on the flat ground. I wasn't amazing at geography, but I knew one thing – that flag was not English or Irish, it was Spanish. Around it four little fires were blazing. Next to them was an enormous white tent, like the ones you see at circuses. To the right of those fires was a huge stock of wooden boxes and barrels, held together by ropes. Hundreds of people were wandering around doing lots of jobs. In the corner of the campsite was a large group of soldiers talking to each other.

I shivered, and backed away slowly. When I thought I was out of sight I started to run, but a large pile of stones was in my way. I couldn't have a diversion so I ran over them. They made loud clinking noises – I hope the Spanish hadn't heard us. But back in the campsite a ship's boy just like me, called Xavier[1], heard strange crinkly noises up on the cliff, and shouted a warning. Immediately five soldiers on watch followed where his hand was pointing, and scrambled up the vine-covered cliff after me. The boy shot along with them, and they ran with their flaming torches alight in their hands, like fireflies. The chase was on!

---

[1] Pronounced, 'Havier'

When I saw the flickering torchlights behind me I scrambled on as fast as I could through the jungle towards our home. At one point I stopped to push a log out of the way, closely dodging a spear which was thrown at me. I grabbed it and carried on running. Eventually I came out of the jungle and onto the plains. I kept sprinting on and on. I could see Hillside House now. I could hear the soldiers, shouting, cursing and swearing at me. I was getting exhausted, and they were gaining on me. At one point I almost had to stop completely. My stitch was so bad, but when I remembered that this was a matter of life and death I kept running. A flaming arrow passed me. The arrow did not hit me but the flame set fire to my trousers. It was terrible heat – I had to hit my leg to stop it from spreading.

Just then I heard the deafening sound of a cannon firing. For a few dreadful seconds I thought it was aimed at me, but then I realised it hadn't even come from the Spanish soldiers, but our home. The chase had now become a battle.

Chapter 16: The siege of Hillside House

I was running so fast now I could leap over our wall – and that's exactly what I did.

Just as I jumped, a cannon fired past me and hit the Spanish who were chasing me. Two men were struck and fell down to the ground, five leapt to the side and retreated into the bushes, and one took cover by lying flat. At the same time, a fire arrow closely missed my ear as it whizzed past and stuck into our door. Two more arrows flew, this time not from the Spanish but from our side, for I could see Carly on top of the hill with a bow and arrow in her hand. I helped Tom reload the cannon to fire it again. Jude and Finn had control of the second cannon, which was, surprisingly, firing spears as well as shot. The Spanish were held back in the jungle, too afraid to attack.

More fire arrows were shot by the Spanish, coming at us thick and fast. Three hit the ground, not damaging anything, but one hit our wooden door, setting it alight, but Hugo put out the flames with a bucket of water. 'They're trying to burn us out!' yelled Finn as a flaming arrow hit close to his feet.

Hundreds of normal arrows rained down upon us. They were coming from all angles, which showed the Spanish had gone right around us. We were trapped! Luckily not many came into our grounds. Hugo, who was in an exposed area, ran over to our well and, putting his feet into the bucket, held on to the rope. He set the winder off, and went down, down to the water below. I thought he was being a bit of a coward, when the rest of us were in such danger. Suddenly the Spanish started to emerge from the jungle and charged.

A spear came down and struck an empty barrel next to me, inches from my hip. I pulled it out then used it as my primary weapon until I went inside to get a musket. I took cover behind the well, and aimed at a Spanish guard who was charging towards us with a sword and a shield. As I pulled the trigger, the man fell to the ground. Suddenly, to my surprise, an arrow shot straight up it. Attached to the bottom was a little note, which read:

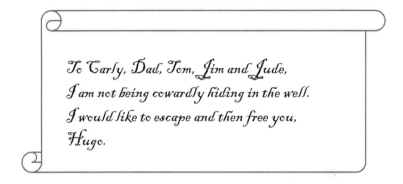

To Carly, Dad, Tom, Jim and Jude,
I am not being cowardly hiding in the well.
I would like to escape and then free you,
Hugo.

Just as I put the note in my pocket, I saw a Spaniard who was just a few metres away, pointing his musket straight at me. He smiled an evil grin, and I knew there was no escape. My last moments had come. Just as his finger began to pull the trigger, there was a fierce bark and Belta leapt at his arm! I ducked down as the man kicked Belta savagely, and the shot went over me. Belta had saved my life, but the Spanish were almost on us!

Out of the bushes, just outside our wall, came two of the Spanish, one fat and one thin, pushing along a small cannon and setting it up to face Hillside House. I tried to stop them by shooting my gun at the cannon, but I had to drop it because another Spaniard who had seen me shot an arrow at me. I leapt back to take cover behind the well, panting. Just then, the Spanish cannon fired, totally demolishing the top part of the well. I dived for cover just in time, but I realised it could not be used for shelter any longer. I retreated behind a pile of dirt, and got my breath back, before peeping around the side and shooting back at the Spanish. Four men came charging down the hill with a battering ram, heading straight for our wall. We were helpless. I had just got into the safety of our home when I heard the crash of the wall – our main defence gone. Another cannon blast hit the side of our home, sending smashed granite everywhere. Dozens of Spaniards came charging in. I looked around: where could I hide? There were two hammocks in the room, four chests, and two barrels – that was it, a barrel! I leapt inside and pulled the lid on after me.

The barrel was marked 'Rum,' and was about a quarter full of the stuff. I could hear the noises of guns shooting, and walls tumbling down outside. This was a battle we had definitely lost: which was hardly surprising, given that there were only six of us and hundreds of Spanish soldiers! A few minutes later, I knew the people were in the same room as I was because I could hear footsteps very close. 'Let's see what's in this barrel,' said one of the men, with a strong Spanish accent. I held my breath and my heart seemed to miss a beat. This was the end.

Chapter 17: Bye bye, Frelser

I breathed a huge sigh of relief when I realised it was the barrel next to me that they were searching. But then I heard the footsteps of the Spaniard coming over to my barrel. He opened the lid slightly and smelt it, but fortunately didn't see me. 'This one's precious rum,' said one. 'Good,' replied the other, 'let's seal it up and take it to the ship for a big party tonight, after our new prisoners are safely away!" he said with an evil laugh. Oh no! They had caught my friends – what could I do now? But they probably hadn't got Hugo – the Spanish wouldn't venture down the remains of a well. I hoped he was all right and could escape from the broken well and rescue us.

I felt them secure the lid of the barrel. It made the whole thing shake. Then they lifted it up. 'Heavier than usual!' I heard one of the grunt. 'We might have to roll it,' said another. They placed me back down on the ground. 'Yea, let's do that,' his mate replied. 'But let's first get these other barrels, too – there's five, and also bottles, so we'll need some help.'

A few minutes later there was a jolt and suddenly the whole thing started to roll. I tried to crawl the opposite direction, but after half a minute I got tired, so stopped for a rest. Immediately I slid backwards, but before I went upside down I hit my head on the side. I put both hands on my head to stop it from bleeding, but the whole thing started again. The rum was splashing all around me, soaking my clothes and going up my mouth and nose. I had to try hard not splutter. About ten minutes later I heard one of the Spaniards say, 'We need some boats to move these to the ship – I think there are some ready where we landed.' 'There's some on the beach,' another one grunted. 'Good,' said one, and we set off again. About an hour later I felt the barrel roll over soft sand, before being hauled into a boat. I was battered and bruised all over, so it was a relief to be gently bobbing along on the sea. I started soothing my aches and pains, which took a long time because I had hundreds of them.

Eventually we stopped bobbing up and down, and someone said, 'These barrels will have to be lifted up by ropes. Let's get the heavy one done first.' I felt them lift me up, and put me back down again with a bump. That must have meant they put the ropes under the barrel. I was hauled up through the air, then everything was still. I was on the deck of the Spanish galleon.

A few hours later I knew from the temperature that night had fallen. The Spanish were singing sea shanties, dancing to music, and getting drunk. I listened for some hours, and eventually everything fell silent – no one was moving. I took the small penknife out of my pocket, and made a little hole out of the barrel which I could peep through. There, in the middle, was a huge table covered by a silk tablecloth laid beautifully. I could see Jude and Tom both tied to the mast, one at either side. Next to me was a barrel and two boxes. Then I heard a scraping sound – I was absolutely petrified. It was coming from next to me, and seemed to be getting closer and closer towards me. Suddenly the blade of a knife went straight through the wall of my barrel. I dodged it quickly – who on earth was making it? I was pretty sure that a barrel was next to me. The knife cut out a hole through both barrels. There was Hugo grinning at me – he was obviously hiding in the next barrel.

"I'm going to get out of my barrel with the strong knife I've got, then I'll open yours," said Hugo. I could hear him scraping then cut away at the lid of my barrel. Soon I was out and we cautiously looked around. There was nobody on the poop deck, and no sign of the Spanish at all except for some drunk sailors sleeping heavily. We crept over to Jude and Tom, and cut the ropes which were tying them up. 'Where are the others?' whispered Hugo, anxious about his family. 'Carly and Finn were taken into the cell behind us,' he answered, pointing to some iron bars.' We tiptoed over, but the cell was locked and there seemed to be no way to open it – our little knives would be useless.

We found a rope lying on the deck, and attached it to the strong iron bars. We tied the other end of the rope to a barrel, in which we (carefully!) placed some cannon balls. We pushed it over the side – it fell for a bit, then hung there. Slowly but surely we could see the iron bars creaking and cracking. We stood back. Suddenly, the barrel crashed down into the sea, taking the iron bars with it and leaving a gaping hole inside the prison cell. Finn and Carly stepped out of the dark cell, but at the sound of the crash one of the sleeping sailors groaned and opened his eyes, and saw Carly right in front of him shaking with terror. His bloodshot eyes stared at her. As he roared with fury to alert his shipmates, we realised what it was too late to escape, and knew what was going to happen. We grabbed all the weapons we could see, cutlasses and pistols. A new battle had begun.

Chapter 18: Gaining the upper hand

At the sound of the shout, two strong men who had been sleeping on the deck stood up and glared at Carly. One raised his pistol. Hugo, who was very protective of his sister, threw a lantern at the man. It fell into his shoe – the man hopped around screaming, 'My foot's on fire, help!' before jumping overboard. While the man was running around the deck, the other man fled, so it was safe to give Carly a pistol. All the commotion meant that from every part of the ship the Spaniards were waking and heading towards us.

I knew how to handle a sword from my time aboard the *Golden Dolphin*. Hugo, who had a cutlass in his hand, knew what I was thinking. I threw Hugo my pistol, which he exchanged for his cutlass. We were both armed and ready to fight. Jude and Tom were frantically firing at the Spaniards swarming down from the poop deck, where Finn was battling more Spaniards. At one point, Tom knocked off the ship's wheel, so the ship could not be steered. Meanwhile, on the other hand, I was sword fighting between boxes and barrels. The sailor I was battling was a strong, bald, sunburned man with a tight belt stuffed with knifes, pistols and keys. He was a skilled dueller so I had to constantly duck and lunge at him to get anywhere near his body. At one point, when I ducked, he missed me and sliced in half a barrel of apples. I picked one up and threw it at one of the Spanish, who was coming out of a stairway. He fell down on another Spaniard, who fell on another, and they ended up as a heap on the floor. We then moved into an open area on the deck, where we engaged in proper swordfighting. There was a barrel on the deck, which I kicked towards him. At that point he was crouching down to dodge my cutlass, so he ended up in the barrel. I quickly placed the lid on, and then tightened it up, before heaving the thing overboard.

Carly, on the other hand, was not doing so well. The

second she got the pistol I passed to her, a Spaniard shot a bullet at her, hitting the gun and knocking it out of her hand. The next thing she knew, she was face to face with a fat man with a knife in each hand. She stepped backwards. The man stepped forwards. She took another step backwards, and he stepped forwards again. They carried on this sequence, until Carly reached the side of the boat. Hugo, who had seen everything happen and was fighting a Spaniard in the crow's nest, and who again wanted to protect his sister, placed the knife he was holding into his mouth and held on to the rope. He swung down, and as he swung closer towards the Spaniard, Carly was now climbing up to the end of the cannon hanging over the edge of the ship. Just as she thought it was all over, her brother seemed to swing from nowhere, his outstretched legs knocking the man over the side of the ship into the sea!

As Hugo climbed back up the rigging, I ran over to help Carly get back from the cannon, and turned around to see a fierce, evil-looking man with glasses, a hook instead of his right hand, a long pointed nose, and a patch over his left eye. I didn't know what to do. All I had was a small knife, as I had lent my pistol to Carly. I could see she had a plan, so I pretended to be a distraction. I ran around the barrels, jumping over boxes, and climbing over mountains of fruit, while Carly worked on loading the cannon. I tried to keep him going around in circles, but eventually I saw all was ready. As Carly took careful aim, I dived for cover next to a container of walrus tusks and pelts. Then I heard the roar of the cannon, and the Spaniard was sent flying overboard and the shot made a hole about the size of a watermelon in the side of the captain's cabin. As I ran to the ammunition storage, which was on the deck, I had to dodge the barrels which the Spaniards were pushing over the poop deck at me. We were outnumbered and were losing the battle.

I ran down some steps and was shocked to see a bunch

of scrawny prisoners behind iron bars. 'Let us out,' one shouted in a voice which sounded strangely familiar, pointing to a key on the wall. I looked more closely, and saw it was Simon Macdonald, the artilleryman from *The Golden Dolphin*! I grabbed the key and unlocked the gate. But there was no time for tender reunions, because just then two Spaniards ran down the steps after me. Simon, along with the other prisoners, who included sailors from *The Golden Dolphin* like Andrew Capuchin, Erik Eriksen, as well as some other men I did not recognise, rushed at the Spaniards and overwhelmed them. They took their weapons and surged onto the deck to help us, furiously taking revenge on the men who had imprisoned them. The prisoners also included Henry Martyn and Marmaduke DeQuincy, *The Golden Dolphin's* chaplain and surgeon. They were men of peace, so went to help the wounded rather than fight themselves.

I went back onto the deck and reloaded my pistol and shot a bullet into the air, before grabbing a cutlass. I fired at a group of Spaniards who were coming out of the door under the poop deck. As I was climbing the ropes up to the crows' nest, I saw that there were three Spaniards following me. I looked in my pocket, what could I use? I eventually found just the thing - an old pistol with no bullets that even had cobwebs on it. The mould and grime stopped the mechanism from working, so I threw it down at the Spaniards who were coming up after me. It hit the first one who fell, knocking his comrades down with him onto the deck. Soon they were trampled by Spaniards, rolled over by barrels, and squashed by boxes as Tom, Jude, Carly, Finn and the recently freed prisoners fought bravely on, although Tom looked like he was badly injured and no one was without cuts and bruises. From where I was clinging to the mast, I could see everything which was happening on the ship and that's when I noticed it. There were fewer Spaniards coming into battle now, so that meant we were getting the upper hand. I could smell victory!

Chapter 19: Farewells, reunions, and victory

I climbed up the remaining eleven rope layers, before I was in the crow's nest. I looked around – where was Hugo, whom I'd come up to help? At least I knew one thing – the person Hugo was trying to fight was there, with his bow and arrow aimed straight at me. He was an evil looking man, with a moustache, long legs and arms, and a small, plump body. His unkempt hair was like a black forest, and a long scar ran across his forehead. He had two bruises on each knee, looking as though someone had splashed them with grey paint. But they were just minor details: the main problem for me was his sharp arrow pointing straight at me, strung on an unrealistically large bow. I didn't know what to do, and there was no Belta to save me now. I decided to take cover behind the mast. It was a risky idea because my limbs were sticking out, but it was probably the best defence. The arrow struck my boot and I felt a stab of pain. I yelled and then grabbed my foot before pulling the arrow out. My foot was bleeding, but I was sure I could win this battle.

I felt in my pockets, but there was nothing. The only thing that could possibly help me was the arrow. I looked around the edge of the mast, and the Spaniard was busy taking another arrow out of his quiver and stringing it in his bow. This was my moment! With all my power, which was weakened due to the pain and blood loss in my foot, I threw the arrow at the man. He yelled like I did, then lost his grip and fell down onto the deck below.

I ripped off my short sleeve and wrapped it around my wound. Now the Spaniard was out the way, I could see Hugo in the smaller of the three crows' nests. This was now my chance to look down and see how the battle was going. My eyes were drawn to the swordfight which was happening between Tom and another Spaniard. I was worried about Tom – he was getting dangerously close to the edge of the ship.

Hugo saw what I was looking at and followed my gaze. We both started to desperately clamber down the rigging to help. But it was too late – Tom had gone.

The Spaniard Tom had been battling was the last one standing on the deck, and we all went for him. He was outnumbered and surrendered. Andrew Capuchin was only too willing to lead him down to the dungeons and lock him up. The last remaining Spanish had jumped into a small boat and were rowing furiously to the island to escape us. We had won the battle and captured the ship!

But this victory had come at a terrible cost.

All over the deck we could hear the groans of wounded men, and see some lying still. Marmaduke DeQuincy and Henry Martyn were busy seeing to the bodies and souls of both our injured and the wounded Spaniards, treating them kindly even though they were our enemies. But it was not just the sick we were worried about. Some men we couldn't save. They were Harry Marmoset, Steve Thin, and my dear friend Tom Ironside. Nine Spanish had also passed away in the battle. That evening, while some of the men we had freed from the Spanish worked on repairing the ship, the rest of us sadly rowed the small boats over to Frelser, carrying the dead bodies with us. Henry Martyn ordered the funeral to take place on the sand dunes, and we buried the bodies in a small graveyard we created, twelve stones marking the spot. We committed the souls of the dead to the Lord, and sailed away, leaving the Spanish who had escaped as the new masters of Frelser. They were welcome to have Hillside House, but would have some repair jobs to do first after all the damage they had inflicted.

As we were leaving, I felt like we were missing something. As we rowed off in the little boat towards the ship, with Jude ordering everyone to go faster, I heard a faint barking and a squawking, and turned round to see Belta on the shore! I shouted, 'Stop!' Jude, who was commanding the boat, looked at me in surprise. 'We're missing Belta and Flash,' I shouted again, 'we've got to go back, Belta saved my life!' 'Turn the boats around,' barked Jude. And so we did. 'Row!' he shouted, 'like you've never rowed before.' 'I think he must have had the whiskey again,' whispered Erik to Henry.

As we came to a shallow part of the beach I rolled up my trousers and leapt out of the boat, as did Jude. 'Flash!' he shouted, 'Belta!' I called. Belta ran towards me and knocked me into the sea as she jumped at me for joy. When she had calmed down, I lifted her into the boat, and could see a wound where she had been kicked by the Spanish soldier in the battle. Marmaduke said he could heal her. There was no sign of our panda, but it was not safe to go looking for her with the Spanish somewhere on the island. With my trusty dog, who had saved my life, we left Frelser. I hoped that I would never see it again.

Back on the ship, we had found charts of these waters. Although our navigator, Tom, had died, one of the English prisoners I didn't know, called Frank Grill, could navigate, and he said he could guide us to a nearby friendly island under British rule, Saint Gabriel. We longed to be back in safety, but if we thought they'd welcome us, we were in for a terrible shock.

Chapter 20: An unpleasant welcome

Jude, who by everyone's agreement had taken command of the ship, ordered the anchor to be raised and the grand ship was off. This Spanish galleon, called *Reina Isabella,*[2] was much larger and grander than *The Golden Dolphin*. It was a more comfortable way to travel, for I suspect that this ship was made for the Spanish queen herself.

I was ordered by Jude to explore the ship. Just under the deck there was a lovely lounge, which was the start of a corridor with all of the cabins leading off. At the end of the corridor there was a ladder down to the second and third layers and then the base of the hull. I went down to the hull and found a storeroom with a huge, arched oak door leading off it. The room was full of barrels, boxes, and cages, which were stores of food, tools, weapons, animals and luxuries. We wouldn't starve on this voyage! I called some sailors to help and we carried some of the supplies onto deck, and had the best feast we had had since *The Golden Dolphin* sank – cheese, bread, biscuits, salads, platters, chicken legs, nuts, dried fruit, gallons of water, smoked maceral, salted beef, luxury chocolates, Turkish delight, gravy, roast potatoes, roast carrots and salted peanuts all washed down with wine and rum. For the next four days we made good progress sailing towards Saint Gabriel. We ate like kings, took turns to help sail the ship, and rested well.

On the morning of the fifth day since we left Frelser, I wondered back down to the store room, and examined the arched door at the back. It was locked, and although I tried to push it in it was far too heavy. What could be behind such a strongly guarded door? I knew there must be keys somewhere for it, but I didn't understand why. But I guessed it couldn't

[2] Trans: *Queen Isabella*, Queen of Castille, whose marriage to Ferdinand of Aragorn united the two parts of Spain.

be just an ordinary store room. Where could the keys be? I tried to remember – did I ever see some on this boat? I thought back to the start of the battle, and suddenly remembered the bald man I was fighting. In his belt he had a sword, a knife, a pistol and something else – a bunch of keys! I furiously climbed back up the ladder and ran down the corridor to the deck where we had been fighting in the barrels. I went to the cell where the prisoners were being kept, and recognised him immediately. He still had the keys on his belt, so I ordered him to give them to us.

Quickly, I went back down to the door and tried the heavy keys. My hand shook as I turned the lock. It made a loud clinking noise, and echoed around the hull. I held my lantern tighter than ever as I slowly and carefully pulled the iron handle. The lock was rusty and the thick door was hard to push open. The iron handle made the door even heavier. Obviously it hadn't been opened in a while, and was designed to stop people getting in. What could it be?

I gasped when I saw it. There were mountains of it. Stacked high and low. All around me. An amazing sight. I was surrounded by stacks of gleaming, glistening gold bullion. We had become instant millionaires. I ran up and told the others, who were as amazed and delighted as me. We stood there, in the hold, daydreaming about the future, when we heard Hugo, who was in the crow's nest, gave a shout, 'land ahoy!' We were approaching Saint Gabriel – Frank had navigated well.

We all ran on deck and looked. We smiled, we were so relived. After a year and a half since we sailed from Ireland, this was the first time we had had any communication with England. They even fired a cannon to greet us! The cannonball flew just above our heads before crashing into the sea just behind our ship, drenching us with water and rocking our ship. Two more cannons fired: one was short, and the other smashed through our rigging snapping one of the masts. They were trying to sink us! We were yelling in panic and waving at them to stop, but we were too far away for them to hear us. I was the first person to realise why: 'the Spanish flag is still flying!' I yelled. We had forgotten to lower it when we captured the ship. 'Get that Spanish rag down!' roared Jude, 'and raise a white one!' 'We don't have one,' screamed Frank, in reply. 'Find something white – sheets, cloths, anything' yelled back Jude in a panic, as a cannonball smashed into the prow and knocked off the figurehead. I ran down and stripped a sheet from the captain's cabin, and sprinted back up on deck waving it. Hugo grabbed it and shot up the damaged rigging, flying it from the top mast. One more cannon ball came, falling short again, before the guns stopped. We were safe.

Immediately Jude ordered us to lower the anchor, and set out with some of us on a small wooden boat towards the port. I joined them. It took us five minutes to reach the port, and the governor, Sir Walker Howarth, came out to meet us with a detachment of soldiers close behind. Jude walked forwards to the side of the boat, towards the governor, and explained our story. When the governor realised we were not Spanish, but English and Irish, he was delighted and asked us to sail the ship into the harbour, but requested that Jude stay on land because he wanted to chat to him. Soon the badly-damaged *Reina Isabella* was safely in port and anchored down, and at last we relaxed to be back on English soil.

Sir Walker sat us down to a big feast while his workers prepared a new ship for us, a great frigate called *The Victoria*. Frank Grill was actually born on this island and wanted to stay here and buy a house with his share of the gold, so the governor provided us with a new navigator for the journey home, Lionel Tiger. The 15,000 thousand-mile journey home was uneventful. After all the dangers we had been through, we were glad to have a quiet voyage and see our homeland again. We didn't know whether to laugh or cry when we finally set eyes on home again.

Epilogue: 25 years later

I was visiting the old port of Dublin for the first in many years. I had come to see the launch of *The Golden Dolphin II*, from the very same harbour that the *Golden Dolphin* had sailed on that fateful voyage a quarter of a century ago. But there was one difference. This harbour was now owned by my old friend Jude Thompson himself. For from his share of the money, he bought two ships and a small port, which slowly expanded until he owned the whole of this harbour and one of the largest fleets of ships in the country. I had come as his guest to see his newest ship launch.

'Jim Ferguson!' I heard a strong voice call. I turned round, and there was Jude himself, coming towards me. He was now 54, with a great brown bushy beard and wore fine clothes. I walked over and we shook hands and embraced. 'Come on, let's sit down and talk, Jim,' he said, pointing to a wooden table. There were no seats so Jude sat on a crate of beer, and I sat on an old apple barrel that looked like it had been sitting there for decades.

We soon got into a long conversation about the old times on board the original *Golden Dolphin* and on Frelser. Although I had done a lot since then, and was now a strong, rich man myself, it was still the adventure of my life. We started talking about all the people who had returned with us on the *Reina Isabella*. 'Carly, her husband and children came over to my house a few weeks ago,' I said. 'She told us that her Dad had used his gold to set up a school for surviving in the wild, and had sent us all to a good school, for they were going to be the next owners of the company.' 'Really?' remarked Jude. 'Yes, I was surprised myself when I heard it,' I replied. 'Are you still in touch with anyone?'

'Oh yes,' said Jude, 'I think everyone who survived the battle on the galleon. And of course, we'd also found that some other members of the crew survived – including Simon Macdonald, Arthur Scarface, Archie Willis, Jason Sharpe and Erik Eriksen. They were picked up by a Dutch clipper and came back here ahead of us. Simon worked with Andrew Capuchin and set up a successful smithy in London. Archie used his money to marry his childhood sweetheart, Beatrice, and they had many children and have just had their first grandchild. And I also think Erik returned to Denmark.' 'Yes, I heard he used his gold to set up a farm,' I added. 'When I am ill I go to see Marmaduke DeQuincy,' I continued. 'He lives close to me in London, where he established what has become a famous private doctor's surgery in Harley Street.'

'Wow,' replied Jude. 'Do you remember Henry Martyn, the chaplain? He used his share of the gold to set up an orphanage, and became minister of church in Yorkshire. But he suffered from ill health, due to the cold and mist of the North. He missed the warm climate of the south seas, and went back to saint Gabriel and became pastor of the church there.'

'He wasn't the only of us to go back,' I added. 'You remember those delicious purple fruits we found on Frelser? Well, Sir Charles Robinson took some home, and it turns out they were unidentified. He wrote a scientific paper on them and called them "dragon fruit." He returned to Frelser – which is now a British island, with a thriving port town – and established a dragon fruit plantation. He sells them all over the world. He lives in London, and has become a Member of Parliament.'

'That's great,' remarked Jude. But it didn't go well for everyone. 'Apparently Jason Sharpe lost all his money gambling and drinking.'

'Oh,' I murmured. 'And of course, Arthur Scarface (who had bullied me and Belta), was arrested for trying to steal wages and gold from other sailors. It can't go well for everyone.' That made me think about how I'd spent my share of the wealth I had found in the ship's hold. After I had got home, I used the money to help my family and go to school, which I'd never had the opportunity to do before because we'd been so poor. But after a while I got bored, and went to see Jude to ask if I could work for him. He promoted me to Able Seaman, and I went on many more frigate trips all around the world. I had lots of adventures, and became one of the most famous sailors in the kingdom, and was eventually promoted to captain of my own ship, which I named, of course, *Frelser*. Belta came with me all the time until she became too old. I was heartbroken when she died, but she had puppies and two of them, one called Belta after her mother and the other named Tom after Tom Ironside, still sail with me today.

As I left the port, I looked back, and saw a small girl creep onto *The Golden Dolphin II* and hide in a barrel. I smiled – I knew the adventures had begun again.

The End